Young Henry
and the
Dragon

Jeanne Kaufman
Illustrated by Daria Tessler

Young Henry went adventuring through woodlands dark and vast, and found himself away from home with daylight fading fast.

He had no heat to warm his toes,
no flame to boil his tea.
He had no way to cook his famous
turnip fricassee.

But Henry knew that to the west and slightly to the south, within a cave, there lived a beast with fire in its mouth.

So off he went, on twisted trails
that ended in a glen.
And there, beside a rocky hill,
he found the dragon's den.

Young Henry shouted, "Dragon!
Can you help a traveling squire?
I ask for just a single flame
to light a warming fire."

The ground began to boom and quake
and smoke curled through the air.
A giant beast with scarlet eyes
came rumbling from its lair.

"Begone!" the dragon puffed and growled.
"Begone, or you'll be toast."
It snorted out a little blaze.
"I'll have a squire roast!"

Young Henry saw the dragon snort
and formed a brilliant plan.
If he could make the dragon laugh,
it just might snort again.

So Henry wiggle-wagged his tongue
and gave his ears a jerk.
The dragon cocked its scaly head,
and didn't even smirk.

Then Henry peeked between his knees.
His hat fell off his head.
And in a rather squeaky voice,
"Halloooo there," Henry said.

oung Henry danced a crazy jig,
his nostrils wide and flared.
He jumped up high and crouched down low.
The dragon only stared.

With hands tucked underneath his arms,
and squatting on the ground,
Young Henry quacked just like a duck
and waddled all around.

He pulled his pants up to his chest.
He did a little spin.
He pinched his nose and sang a song.
The dragon didn't grin.

Then Henry tried his favorite joke
(he giggled when he said it) –
What do you get when you cross a dragon with a wild pig?
Smokey the Boar!
The dragon didn't get it.

"Forget it," Henry said. "That's it!"
"I'm done!" he yelled. "I'm through!"
"If you don't think that's funny, well,
there's nothing I can do."

So with a huff, he turned to leave
but tripped upon some roots.
He hit the ground and tumbled,
rolling head right over boots.

A little oak tree stopped him.
It shivered with the shove.
Then acorns, leaves, and tiny sticks
rained down from up above.

From deep inside the leafy pile,
Young Henry heard a squeak.
Was that a giggle? Henry thought.
He took a little peek.

The dragon swayed from side to side
and twitched from head to claw.
A smoking snort escaped its lips,
and then a huge GUFFAW!!

The blaze shot out one hundred feet.
Young Henry took his aim.
He lifted up a knobby stick
and caught the passing flame.

With torch held high, he freed himself.
He had his fire at last!
And while the dragon rolled about,
Young Henry tiptoed past.

Then far off from the dragon's lair,
in daylight's final glow,
Young Henry took his little flame
and watched it pop and grow.

But there, beyond the fire's warmth,
a massive shadow rose,
and Henry shuddered as the smell
of brimstone filled his nose.

The giant beast with scarlet eyes
had found his hiding place.
The dragon stood above him now,
a grimace on its face.

ut, wait! That grimace was a grin!
It clapped its claws together.
"I haven't laughed in 50 years.
I'm feeling so much better!"

They sat beneath the darkened sky
and as the moon rose higher,
Young Henry shared his fricassee
while Dragon stoked the fire.